Dear P

Do you want to spark your child's creativity? Do you want your child to become a confident writer? Road to Writing can help.

Road to Writing is a unique creative writing program that gives even the youngest writers a chance to express themselves. Featuring five distinct levels, or Miles, the Road to Writing program accompanies children from their first attempts at writing to comfortably writing on their own.

MILE 1 — **A Creative Start**
For children who "write" stories by drawing pictures
- easy picture prompts • familiar subjects • places to draw

MILE 2 — **Creative Writing With Help**
For children who write easy words with help
- detailed picture prompts • places to draw and label

MILE 3 — **Creative Writing On Your Own**
For children who write simple sentences on their own
- basic story starters • popular topics • places to write

MILE 4 — **First Journals**
For children who are comfortable writing short paragraphs
- more complex story starters • space for free writing

MILE 5 — **Journals**
For children who want to try different kinds of writing
- cues for poems, jokes, stories • brainstorming pages

There's no need to hurry through the Miles. Road to Writing is designed without age or grade levels. Children can progress at their own speed, developing confidence and pride in their writing ability along the way.

Road to Writing—"write" from the start!

Look for these

Road to Writing

books

Mile 1

Animal Crackers
Cool School
Mostly Monsters
Super Me!

Mile 2

Boo!
Dinosaur Days
Get a Clue!
Road Trip

Mile 3

Barbie: Always in Style
Happily Never After: Tangled Tales
Monkey Business
Sports Shorts

Tips for Using this Book

- Let your child read each page and write a response—right in the book!
- Don't worry about spelling or penmanship. Just let your child enjoy the experience of capturing ideas on paper.
- Remind your child to write at his or her own pace. There's no rush!
- Encourage your child with plenty of praise.

Pencils, pens, and crayons are all suitable for use in this book. Markers are not recommended.

A GOLDEN BOOK • New York
Golden Books Publishing Company, Inc. New York, New York 10106

ISBN: 0-307-45413-4

10 9 8 7 6 5 4 3 2 1

Barbie™ Always in Style

written and illustrated by

(your name)

Barbie and Christie are invited
to a fancy party!

Fill in the card.

Date: ____________

Time: ____________ until ____________

Place: ________________________

R.S.V.P.

____ Yes ____ No

Draw a picture of what YOU would wear to a fancy party.

Barbie is coaching Skipper's soccer team.

Pretend you started a soccer team.

What is your team name?

____

What color are your uniforms?

____

What position will you play?

(Check one.)

_____ Goalie

_____ Sweeper

_____ Wing

_____ Striker

Draw the trophy for the winning soccer team.

Barbie likes to decorate her house.
What are your talents?

Things I do well:

____

____

____

____

____

____

Things I'd like to do better:

Draw yourself doing one of these things.

Barbie needs help running her fashion company.

Design an outfit for her new spring line.

What will you call this outfit?

____

Write a news flash about it.

____

(title of your article)

New York, N.Y.

Barbie & Co. wowed the fashion world today!

Barbie writes in her diary every day.

Write about what happened to you today.

(date)

Dear Diary,

Draw a picture of your favorite thing you did today.

One day, Barbie was walking
in the park.
A dark cloud rolled in.
It started to rain!

Write what happened next.

All of a sudden, ______________________________

____

____

____

Then, ______________________________

____

____

____

Finally, ______________________________

____

____

____

Barbie is starring in a new ballet.
Make a poster for the ballet.

Write a sentence that will make people want to come to the show.

You're going on a trip!
Send Barbie a postcard.

Draw the picture on the front.

Write a message on the back.

Dear Barbie,

From,

To: Barbie

Barbie's friend Teresa has just started a new magazine!

What is the magazine called?

____

Who will buy this magazine?

____

____

Fill in the Table of Contents.

Page 10 "Make Friends–And Keep Them!"

Page 20 ______________________

Page 35 ______________________

Page 50 ______________________

Draw a picture of the first issue.

Stacie needs help making cupcakes.

Write instructions for her.

Step 1:

Step 2:

Step 3:

Step 4:

What does the kitchen look like when Stacie is done?

Barbie was swimming in the ocean.
She saw something ahead.
"Is that a sunken ship?"
she asked herself.

Write the rest of the story.

THE END

Barbie and her friends
are having a sleepover.

What do YOU do at a sleepover?

I bring ______________________.

I eat ______________________.

I play ______________________.

I go to sleep at ______________.

Draw a picture of you
the next morning.

Barbie and Kelly are going to the beach.

Make a list of what they should bring.

1. Flippers

2. Sunscreen

3. ______________________

4. ______________________

5. ______________________

6. ______________________

Draw yourself at the beach.

Barbie has dreamed
of many different careers.
What do you want to do?

Things I want to be when I grow up:

Things I DON'T want to be when I grow up:

Barbie is a famous photographer.

Draw Barbie taking pictures of wild animals in Africa.

Write a story about your picture.

First, ______________________________

____

____

____

Then, ______________________________

____

____

____

Finally, ______________________________

____

____

____

Roses are red.
Barbie loves pink.
Girls can do anything
they want to, I think.

Write your own poem.

Roses are red.
Clovers are green.

Draw a picture to go with it.

Barbie started a scrapbook.

Write the captions for her.
Then draw the pictures.

Barbie, making some ____________________.

Ken, with his friend, ____________________.

Everyone, under the

________________________.

It's springtime!
Barbie is planting flowers.

Write instructions for her.

Step 1: ______________________________

____

____

Step 2: ______________________________

____

____

Step 3: ______________________________

____

____

Step 4: ______________________________

____

____

Draw a picture of the garden all in bloom.

Barbie is a camp counselor.
Help her plan the schedule.

8:00 Breakfast!

10:00 ____________________

12:00 Lunch!

2:00 ____________________

4:00 ____________________

6:00 Dinner!

8:00 ____________________

9:00 ____________________

Design a camp T-shirt
for all the campers to wear.

Christie and Steven are happy when they go hiking.

What makes you happy?

1. ____________________

2. ____________________

3. ____________________

4. ____________________

5. ____________________

Draw yourself doing one of the things on your list.

Barbie is having a pet show.
To win, a pet must be friendly.

What else?

The pet must be . . .

1. ______________________________

2. ______________________________

3. ______________________________

4. ______________________________

Draw a picture of the pet
that wins first prize.

Here's a picture of
Barbie and her sisters.

Draw a picture of you
and your family.